Prim:

A Fairy Tale of an Audacious Girl

KIARA   SHANKAR

&

VINAY   SHANKAR

Library of Congress Control Number: 2019900256

ISBN-13/ISBN:

  978-1-950263-00-4 / 1-950263-00-2 (Paperback - Color Interior)
  978-1-950263-03-5 / 1-950263-03-7 (Paperback - B&W Interior)
  978-1-950263-01-1 / 1-950263-01-0 (Hardcover - Color Interior)
  978-1-950263-02-8 / 1-950263-02-9 (eBook)

First Edition: March 2019. Published by Vinay Shankar, San Ramon, California, USA.

Written by Kiara Shankar and Vinay Shankar.

Visit the authors' website at www.vikipublishing.com

Dedicated to Humanity!

Table of Contents

The Early Life

Once upon a time, in a small wooden cottage in a large dense forest lived a beautiful audacious twelve-year-old girl named Primrose Fernetise. She had long golden hair, big blue eyes, and a pink rosebud mouth. Despite her beauty and having a heart of pure gold, Primrose's family were having serious financial difficulties. Due to their family's financial situation, they couldn't afford to live in the mainland town of Amiablevue and hence they had to live in a deserted forest far away from the city center. Primrose's cottage was an hour wagon ride away from that town.

To make a living, Primrose would stitch cotton clothes and crochet woolen sweaters. Her older brother, Stanley, would chop down trees from the forest and sell them to merchants in Amiablevue. Stanley would carry those heavy wood logs, stitched clothes, and woolen sweaters in their family's dark brown wagon pulled by a white horse named Ginger. Primrose's mother had been fighting a sickness for a long time and had passed away one morning. Primrose, her father, and older brother, Stanley mourned for a few days due to the sudden loss of their beloved family member.

After this terrible loss in the Fernetise family, Stanley had to work for extended hours in the woods and Primrose had to stitch clothes every day while taking care of her dear old father and managing the daily tasks about the house.

As the days passed, one evening when Primrose was making dinner for the family, her father suddenly suffered a stroke, the stroke made him feel terribly ill, and he couldn't talk nor could he move from his bed as the seizure from the stroke caused a severe paralysis on both of his legs.

Primrose and Stanley gave him some medicine made with natural herbs which helped him recover his voice, but his health continued to decline.

Primrose managed to take care of her sick father every day, while Stanley was working hard in the forest to make money for taking care of their family expenses.

After a few days, Primrose's father's health slowly recovered, but his paralyzed legs wouldn't recover. So, he continued to be bedridden and dependent on Primrose and Stanley.

However, Primrose's father was incredibly pleased with the dedicated care and hospitality offered by his daughter and son.

"Primrose, I wish I could go out and help your brother work, but I'm afraid my paralyzed legs won't allow me out of this bed." Primrose's father looked down at his motionless legs, his heart filled with sorrow.

"Don't worry, dear Father. I have an idea! I know a nectar from a divine flower that grows only in the deep forest. I will go to the forest tomorrow morning and try to search for that divine flower. If I somehow find that nectar from the divine flower and have you drink it, it will cure your paralysis," Primrose consoled.

"Thank you, Primrose. I knew I could rely on you for help. That would be a great help for me," Primrose's father replied, with a humble look.

Encounter with the Woodland Animals

The next day at early dawn, Primrose got ready, took a handwoven basket, and headed towards the deep forest, leaving her father alone with Stanley at the cottage. She then walked a couple of miles in the dense forest until she reached a river filled with crystal-clear blue water. Hopping over smooth light gray stepping stones that formed a natural bridge over the river, she made her way across the river.

The river water was so fresh. Primrose bent down and drank handfuls of the pure water to quench her thirst from the long lonely hike in the wilderness she had. Finally, she stood up and ran across a beautiful meadow next to the sparkling river. The meadow was filled with rich green grass, ambient nature sounds, loud chirps from nightingale birds, yellow-and-black buzzing bees, fluttery monarch butterflies, bright colorful flowers, and the strong fragrant aromas of flowers.

When Primrose reached the other end of the deep forest, a group of woodland animals consisting of identical triplet deer, an owl, a rabbit, a squirrel, and a skunk surrounded her, offering her an appetizing variety of fresh berries and nuts. The woodland animals had welcoming looks on their faces.

Primrose was delighted to see a group of woodland animals offering her such bounty.

Thank you! Wow, I never thought animals in the wild forest could be so kind to humans, Primrose thought, surprisingly.

She had never been around animals before except her one—and only—pet gorgeous Ginger.

The woodland animals chuckled, and said:

"Welcome, Primrose!"

Primrose screamed in horror, she was shocked to see the woodland animals talking to her. Primrose felt like her world was tearing apart.

"What's going on?!" Primrose shouted, frightened.

A young, soft-furred white rabbit with dark violet eyes smiled at her with real warmth and said:

"Primrose, we know you are from Amiablevue land on the other side of the forest. We know your mother passed away recently, your father is ill, and your family is living in poverty. Also, you are here in this deep forest to search for nectar from a divine flower in order to cure your father's illness. Am I right?"

Primrose didn't understand completely what the tiny rabbit was purring about, but she was able to grasp what the rabbit had mentioned about her family and she wondered, how the woodland animals knew all about her family's situation.

Primrose sighed and thought:

Have the woodland creatures been stalking me? This rabbit is seriously creepy! How can these woodland animals talk like humans? Maybe, this is just a dream? Primrose pinched herself stiffly unsuccessfully assuring herself.

She panicked and thought:

Well, it's not a dream. Hopefully, these crazy creatures will come back to their senses. Right? Yes or maybe not?

"I don't think your stories about me are realistic. I need to look for divine flower nectar and go back home before it gets dark. So, please don't trouble me right now.

"You and your fairy tale stories seem very funny to me. If you want, you could start your own comedy show in the town. You'll make a lot of money and become the world's most famous comedians ever in animal history," Primrose commented, sarcastically.

The encounter with the woodland animals and their unbelievable stories reminded Primrose of old funny memories of her brother who had acted in Romeo & Juliet stage show when he was thirteen years old. Primrose started to laugh out loud by recalling the mishaps her brother had had during the show, like when he put freshly baked apple pie on the stage director's face by accident. Then there were the times when Stanley flew across his balcony, swinging on a rope and accidently fell into Juliet's hot tub. Juliet's pretend father had been splashed by it and had whacked Stanley on his back with a stick for his ignorant behavior. Poor Stanley had run sprinting away screaming his head off and purposefully ripping Juliet's expensive gown. All of this chaos had the audience throwing spoiled eggs at Stanley, Juliet, and everyone else standing beside Stanley on the stage.

For a minute, Primrose was completely immersed in her funny memories of Stanley from the Romeo & Juliet stage show. After a while, Violet interrupted Primrose in her thoughts by explaining more about the tale the woodland animals were trying to tell her to make her believe them.

"Primrose, more importantly, we also know that you are destined to save the world's population. Many people are becoming ill and dying. You're the only one that can save us all," Violet continued, hopping up and down onto the grassy patch on the edge of the river.

"What do you mean by, 'you're the only one that can save us all,' rabbit? How do you know who I am?" Primrose asked, biting her chapped bottom lip.

The rabbit sighed and said:

"Well, I can't give you a quick answer, but we'll tell you the whole entire story. Before telling you the whole story, let us introduce ourselves to you first. I'm Violet, the genius of all, those triplet deer are Ashlynn, the amazing ballet dancer; Cynthia, the sensational singer; and the ever-artistic Susan. That wise, old, respectful, and judicious owl is Hedwig. Also, the squirrel is Acorn, who is very helpful, and the talented skunk over there is called Pepper. Could you please make us that special herbal tea, Pepper?"

Pepper bobbed her head quickly and scurried inside a wooden shelter near the edge of the river, filled with natural spices, herbs, flowers, water and more that was stored neatly in tiny glass mason jars. Pepper was a huge fan of going green, especially to save the world for future generations. Violet led Primrose and the woodland animals to a large shelter made of wood and covered with green moss. They sat on chopped tree trunks in front of the shelter. As the chatter continued on the front yard of the shelter, Primrose could instantly tell that Violet was the bragger of the group, which was true.

Pepper soon came inside holding a wooden tray placed with old wooden tea cups and a teapot that was filled with hot green tea. The teapot was carved with adorable hearts which Susan said she had made a year ago.

Acorn loved to help out others, which always made her blush deeply with pride, when she was complimented on her skills.

Pepper and Acorn both helped to pour the hot green tea into the wooden cups, and then passed the tea cups around for everyone to enjoy the hot tea. The steam from everyone's cup looked like a foggy mist that was rising high into the air.

"I'm getting a little freaked out looking at all of you making and drinking tea like real human beings and also talking in my human language, could someone please help me understand what is going on?" Primrose yelled, waving her arms in the air, wildly.

"We totally understand your confusion and frustration, Primrose. You definitely have the right to understand who we are and how we could communicate to you in your own human language. We really appreciate your bravery in asking for clarification on your unexpected encounter with us woodland animals, and we'll definitely clarify all your doubts about us, so please be patient," Pepper said, offering a cup of hot green tea to Primrose.

Violet cleared her throat and said:

"Hedwig, why don't you tell her the story about it?"

Hedwig nodded and began.

"Primrose, first of all, did you know how your mother named you after a flower? Let me tell you an interesting story about your inspiring flower name as well. When you were born, an astrologer told your mother that you were a special child and if she named you after a certain gorgeous flower, you would bring good luck to the family when you turned twelve years old, hence she named you after the beautiful flower called Primrose," Hedwig said, stirring his teacup with a small wooden spoon.

"Anyways, coming back to your main question about who we are. We are a group of woodland animals from Mystopical that have extraordinary mystical powers. We try to identify courageous, lionhearted human children who were born with hidden talents that have never been shown to anybody but to themselves. We empower such special, talented human children and collaborate with them in all the mystical, adventurous expeditions that we carry out to save the planet. Also, we work together with them to protect the well-being of all plants, animals, and humans from the evil spirits.

"This is the reason why we chose you for our forthcoming quest since your hidden exceptional abilities meet our requirements and expectations to expeditiously accomplish this important task. Hopefully, this clarifies some of your confusions on how we, a bunch of woodland animals, could possibly know so much information about you and your family's background as well as how we can communicate with you in your language," Hedwig continued, slurping up the last drops of hot green tea.

Primrose sighed and thought: *Aha! Okay, I guess the story from these woodland animals is now making some sense to me, finally!"*

"Okay, thank you for the detailed information and clarification that you have shared, I think I'm getting to a point where I am starting to believe your story, but what is the quest that you are on, Hedwig?" Primrose asked, curiously.

"Good question. Again, Primrose, I liked your curiosity and courage is seeking to understand the proposed action plan," Hedwig replied, softly patting Primrose's shoulder.

"There is an evil sorceress on the dark side of Mystopical. She has a vicious plan to kill every single human and animal in the world. She also has a wicked plan to take away the mystical powers from us, the woodland animals, using an awful evil spell. So, we want to empower your hidden brave human skills with our mystical powers to confront and conquer the evil sorceress in order to save the world from her evil spell."

"Hmm, that sounds interesting, Hedwig! How exactly do I gain my mystical powers?" Primrose asked excitedly.

"I'll give you the sacred flower named Primrose that you are named after. Please come here and touch it, so you can gain all the mystical abilities required to defeat the evil sorceress. Also, we'll all come along with you to guide you every step of the way on this quest to bring down the evil sorceress," Hedwig added, holding the Primrose flower stem in his wing for Primrose to touch.

Primrose tensed up, then she spun around quickly and looked at everyone nervously.

"I know I'm an audacious girl, but I'm a bit apprehensive about this important task. Do you think I will be able to take on this task without having prior experience with any such mystical abilities like you? I don't want to be a failure, attempting the impossible. Are you sure this is a good idea?" Primrose asked, twitching her nose.

"Don't worry about a thing, Primrose. We have done this type of adventure many times in the past. So, this is not our first quest. In addition to that, Hedwig has been studying and experimenting with all kinds of logistics for this expedition. He's quite an expert on it now, especially for what he is trying to protect us with. There is a lot of information and instructions that Hedwig will share with all of us as soon as possible," Ashlynn said, making Primrose ponder even more.

"Okay. Thank you, Ashlynn, for making me feel a bit relaxed. By the way, what's Mystopical?" Primrose asked, to clarify her confusion about the unfamiliar word that Hedwig had mentioned in the beginning.

"Well, Mystopical is a magical world made up of two big islands, located hundreds of miles north of the deep forest. Both good and evil creatures with great mystical powers live in this magical world. Like, woodland animals, munchkins, human mystics, human prophets who practice good deeds also the bad sorcerers and wizards who practice terrible witchcrafts.

"Please do note, however, that you must keep this information confidential otherwise we may face even more obstacles on our quest. The evil side is always watching and waiting," Hedwig said, in a convincing way.

Hedwig pivoted back to describing Mystopical. "Actually, these two big islands in Mystopical are separated by a deep ocean. The island with good creatures is called Heavenvue Island and the other region filled with bad creatures is called Hellevue Island.

To be precise, Heavenvue is the place where we, the woodland animals, and other good creatures like munchkins and human mystics live.

Heavenvue Island is surrounded by the blue sea and it is filled with green forests, breathtaking meadows, gorgeous splashy waterfalls and exquisite nature.

Whereas, the sea next to Hellevue Island is surrounded by dark, inky, deep sea and covered by a murky atmosphere of gloomy clouds.

The bad sorcerers and wizards who practice vicious and cruel acts actually live on haze shrouded Hellevue. In fact, the evil sorceress named Evelyn Velecrona is the queen of the Hellevue Island.

Our mission is to venture into this dreary part of Mystopical to defeat Evelyn using our mystical powers and put an end to her evil spell and save the world.

This is the truth and you have to believe in us, Primrose, because this is our best opportunity to save the world and humanity from bad evil spirits."

"After hearing your detailed explanation, I now truly believe in your mystical abilities and the expedition that you all are undertaking to save the world. I'm certainly honored to be part of such expedition to save humanity and the world, so please count me in!" Primrose exclaimed, touching the supernatural Primrose flower that Hedwig was holding.

The moment she touched the stem of flower, her body felt an experience like she was on top of the world filled with overwhelming ecstasy.

A flash of lightning appeared in the sky followed by a loud rumbling thunder and a colorful rainbow also emerged from the sky.

"Congratulations Primrose, you have been blessed and granted with magical abilities like us!" Violet reaffirmed, pointing both of her paws towards the beautiful rainbow that had just formed across the sky.

"Thank you, everybody!" Primrose said, blissfully.

"You are welcome, Primrose!" Acorn cheered, on behalf of everyone.

"Looks like a bad storm is expected in the coming days due to a change in the season, we should expedite our mission, Hedwig," Cynthia said, alerting the other woodland animals and Primrose.

"That's right, Hedwig!" Ashlynn and Susan exclaimed at the exact same time, looking at each other and nodding.

"Let's get our supplies for the journey and load them into the boat!" Acorn exclaimed, handing everyone a woven basket.

As soon as the baskets were filled with food and other essential supplies needed for the journey, Susan, Acorn, Ashlynn, and Violet helped load them into a large wooden boat. Everyone except Primrose had exited the shelter and started to climb aboard the boat.

"Wait, the reason I came into this deep forest in the first place was to get nectar from a divine flower to heal my father's sickness. Um, shouldn't I cure my father first, before we go on this mission?" Primrose asked, hesitating to board the boat.

Hedwig continued saying, "I agree but there is one more important thing I need to tell you, Primrose.

"Evelyn has put curse on all humans, including you.

"So, first you must break that curse by defeating Evelyn and her evil powers. Only then can you heal your father," said Hedwig, in a convincing manner.

"Also, one more thing that I would like to disclose with you is, once we succeed in bringing down the evil sorceress with our mystical powers, we can promise you that a few great things are going to occur immediately following the demise of the evil queen, Evelyn. Those prospective great things are, first and foremost the existing evil curse on humanity will be broken. Health, wellness of nations will thrive; your father's sickness will be cured; your family situation will prosper; and last but not least, we will try to use our mystical powers to resurrect your mother's life."

Primrose was pleased with what Hedwig had just proposed. She couldn't believe how blessed she was to have had such a promising mystical encounter with these woodland animals.

Primrose thought to herself, *"Oh dear God! I feel so blessed, please help me succeed on this critical task of breaking the evil curse on humanity and please..., please..., please help bring my beloved mother back to life!"*

She ran out of the shelter and boarded the boat.

"All aboard! Off we go!" Pepper hollered, rowing the boat gently down the river.

Meeting with the Munchkins

After sailing down the blue river for a while, Primrose began to get confused about how to get to the island.

"Does this river take us all the way to Mystopical?" Primrose asked, curiously.

"Certainly not, Primrose! Sailing on this long mighty river for a few miles will take us to the estuary where the river meets with the ocean, then we have to sail further on the deep ocean for a couple of days to reach Heavenvue," Hedwig said, clarifying Primrose's confusion.

"When we reach Heavenvue, let's go to Wildwood Bakery for lunch and ask the munchkins for some advice," Violet announced, clearing her throat.

"Where exactly is Wildwood Bakery? Also, who or what are munchkins?" Primrose asked, full of confusion.

"The munchkins come from Munchville, a small kingdom located in the eastern part of Heavenvue. Munchkins are like funny looking, dwarf people who are always dressed up in fairy-tale costumes. They also have mystical abilities like us to some level," Violet said, softly.

"Also, let's show them Hedwig's magical mirror that told us that Primrose was destined to be the savior of humanity," Acorn added, smiling.

Everyone nodded and the boat began to fill with happy chatter. They all told funny stories about themselves, sang, danced, cracked jokes and had great fun as they sailed to Munchville.

After sailing on the ocean for a couple of days, their boat finally arrived at Munchville. They all got off the boat and headed towards the Wildwood Bakery on the oceanfront street.

"Hey, Jax! How are you, my friend!" Violet shouted and rushed toward a purple curly haired munchkin, to give him a big warm hug.

"I'm doing great! Thanks for asking! How are you? Long time no see!" Jax said, giving them a long grin.

Jax continued greeting them, "It's nice to meet you and your friends, Violet! How may I help you today?"

Violet and her friends started describing to Jax the complete story about Primrose and the magical mirror to seek his kind advice.

"Well, let's first have some lunch that I and my colleagues have prepared for our Wildwood Bakery customers, then we will discuss this matter. After that, we must head over to the Crazy Cake Cottage where my grandmother lives. She will be able to share some advice with you guys," Jax said, firmly.

Everyone nodded and followed Jax to a large dining table to enjoy a delicious lunch. Everybody including Ashlynn, Susan, Cynthia plopped onto the red velvet cushioned dining chairs and yelled: "Hey! These chairs are as fluffy as cumulus clouds!"

Jax and his other munchkin colleagues served them many specialty food made with lots of sugar such as sweet caramelized rose petals, cotton candy marshmallows filled with melted dark chocolate, honey-coated biscuits, candied violets, crispy butter buns, creamy s'more milkshakes made with mint and mocha, also cold vanilla mochi ice cream as a final dessert.

Everyone enjoyed the yummilicious lunch so much, they began to lick off the food leftovers on their messy mouths.

After finishing the dessert, they all helped Jax clean up the table.

"Thank you for the wonderful meal, Jax," Primrose said, gratefully.

"It was quite delicious, if I say so myself. I've never had a sugary meal like this, my whole entire life."

"I would second that! Jax is the most well-known culinary expert throughout all of Munchville," Violet said, praising Jax's pastry mastery.

Jax felt delighted and said:

"You are welcome, Primrose and Violet! I'm glad you guys liked it. I'm a baker, after all, and it's my responsibility to feed our hungry customers."

Everyone freshened up and then set off towards the Crazy Cake Cottage. After a mile walk on a rocky trail, they reached the cottage.

Jax embraced his grandmother with a big warm hug.

"Hello, Grandmother! I came here with some of my friends to visit you. It looks like they need some help from you," Jax said, smiling.

"A friend of my beloved Jax, is a friend of mine. Now, how may I help you, dearies?" Mrs. Walters said sweetly, looking at Primrose and the woodland animals.

Stepping forward, Pepper began to tell the entire story—from their planned expedition to their responsibility to save humanity.

"But please keep this information confidential," Pepper pleaded, putting her paws together.

"Of course, Pepper. I will keep this confidential. Now, may I see that magical mirror?" Mrs. Walters asked, kindly.

Hedwig handed her the magical mirror and then gently sprinkled a shade of dark green powder on it. The powder vanished into the glass and began hissing loudly.

"Knock it three times and you can see what Evelyn is up to," Hedwig said to Mrs. Walters.

"Evelyn? Sorry, but who's Evelyn again?" Primrose asked, curiously.

"That's the same evil sorceress that we've told you before," Acorn explained, laughing.

"Sorry, Acorn. I forgot about that. Please excuse my poor memory," Primrose said, meekly.

Mrs. Walters knocked three times on the magical mirror and suddenly Evelyn's holographic image started to appear on the mirror. She was in her dark haunted castle.

There was gray mist everywhere, with bats flying all over the place.

Evelyn was wearing a black dress and a matching cape decorated with dry glitter glue and had her wavy orange hair down to her shoulders. She was wearing dark red lipstick with black furry boots, while holding a long dark brown spell-casting wand.

"What a monstrous look she has!" Mrs. Walters mumbled, terrified.

The group continued to glance at Evelyn's horrendous appearance in the magical mirror.

"Did you know? Nearly half of the population of world has been obliterated with my powerful spell, Baxter," Evelyn said, seemingly annoyed.

"I know, madam Evelyn," the black crow grimed, firmly sitting on her arm.

"I will conquer and rule the ugly Heavenvue of Mystopical, maybe soon I'll rule the whole world. All I have to do is wipe out the entire human and animal population on the face of the earth!" Evelyn cackled, waving her spell casting wand in the air. In the reflection of the moonlight, the woodland animals saw her scary green eyes twinkling with cruelty.

After a moment, the mirror turned clear and Evelyn's appearance slowly faded away.

"Wow, this is one dangerous and life-threatening mission we are taking on. Dealing with an evil witch may come with serious consequences, I suppose..." Ashlynn said, her voice trailing off.

"Don't you worry about a thing, Ashlynn! I will guide you all every step of the way until we accomplish our mission to bring down this cruel queen," Hedwig concluded, gently patting Ashlynn on the back.

"Who's is that crow and why is it sitting on her hand?" Primrose blurted out, with interest.

"He's Evelyn's evil pet crow, whose persona is as cunning as Evelyn. We only have a few days left for the epic journey to Hellevue!" Hedwig said, worried.

"Now, Mrs. Walters, the reason why we are here to meet you today is that we are looking for a shortest sea-route map. We are also looking for a larger ship since our small boat may not be able to handle the severe ocean weather conditions en route to Hellevue Island. Violet had mentioned that the munchkins may have the sea-route map to get to Hellevue faster. Is it possible for you to share with us the map of Mystopical world? Also, do you know anyone from Munchville who could lend us a large ship for our voyage?" Cynthia said, requesting Mrs. Walters help.

"Okay, let me think about that," Mrs. Walters replied, swiftly tapping her index finger on her chin.

After a few minutes, an idea suddenly popped up in her mind.

Mrs. Walters replied, "Let's go meet the queen of Munchville in the Sweet Palace. I'm certain that she will have a map of Mystopical, and she could probably lend you a large ship to sail across the mystical ocean. You'll definitely need a large ship to make it through the dark, inky, deep sea to reach the Hellevue Island."

"We must go to the royal Sweet Palace, before it's too late!

Let's go, everybody!" Mrs. Walters said, leading everyone out the door.

Attending Queen Sarah's Marriage

Everyone exited the cottage and headed towards the royal Sweet Palace.

Jax faced a munchkin soldier at the fort's main gate and said:

"Dear Soldier, our woodland friends from the other side of the forest are here to meet Queen Sarah. Would you please let us in?"

"Sorry, the queen of Munchville is not available for any meeting with munchkins or any visitors until next week because she is busy with her marriage preparations. I would suggest you all come back a week from now," the soldier replied.

"This is an urgent matter! Our woodland friends are on a critical mission to protect humanity. They need our majesty, Queen Sarah's help urgently and we would appreciate if you could let us in today," Mrs. Walters pleaded.

After listening to Mrs. Walter's kind requesting words, the soldier was convinced to let Mrs. Walters, Jax, Primrose and all the woodland animals inside the Sweet Palace to meet with Queen Sarah.

As soon as the team entered the great hall of the Sweet Palace, the doorkeeper at the entrance of the royal hall welcomed the team and helped them make their way to Queen Sarah's golden throne room.

"Enjoy your visit here, folks," the doorkeeper said, returning back to the door entrance.

The queen was sitting on her golden throne, gazing out the window. The team slowly walked a few steps closer to the dais and everyone bowed down to Queen Sarah to show her respect.

Jax bowed and said:

"Good afternoon, your highness. Me and my grandmother came with some of our friends to meet you; they need your help."

The queen adjusted her furry outfit and said with a huge smile:

"Okay, thanks for coming all the way to seek my help. Now do tell me, what can I do for you all?

Mrs. Walters explained to Queen Sarah in detail the story of the woodland animals, Primrose's curse, and their planned expedition to the Hellevue Island to bring down the evil sorceress named Evelyn Velecrona. Also, to bring back peace, well-being and happiness to humanity.

"Your highness, may we ask your help? We need the map of Mystopical, and we would also appreciate if you could lend us a big ship and a few soldiers to succeed in our task," Hedwig requested to Queen Sarah on behalf of the group.

"Very impressive! Since you folks are endeavoring to protect the well-being of humanity from the evil spirits, I will definitely help you accomplish your mission, I will ask my chief commander of the army, Major Frederick, to arrange all the necessary assistance you may need for this incredible mission," Queen Sarah replied, amazed by their risky journey to save humanity.

"That's very kind of you, Queen Sarah! We can't thank you enough for your kindness and help!" Hedwig said, gratefully.

Everyone nodded and bowed down again to second what Hedwig had said to Queen Sarah and to express their appreciation.

Queen Sarah continued. "You are most welcome. By the way, tonight there is a marriage reception dinner. I invite you all to stay in the royal guest house overnight and attend the dinner party. You may start your journey tomorrow morning."

Mrs. Walters, Jax, Hedwig and all of the others in the group thanked Queen Sarah from the bottom of their hearts for her kind hospitality and great assistance.

"I will take these folks to the royal guest house to freshen up, your highness," one of her butlers offered.

The butler showed them the way to the guest house. Everyone walked towards the guest house that was a few steps across the big royal garden. The garden was filled with red, white, yellow and pink roses, which were Queen Sarah's favorites.

The fresh scented aroma coming from roses and other flowers in the garden was refreshing and pleasant.

"Here are your room keys, mates. This guest house has all the best amenities, so please enjoy your stay tonight. I will take care of all your belongings," the butler said, handing Cynthia the room keys.

"Thank you, Sir. We appreciate your help," Mrs. Walters said.

Hedwig handed his sack over to the butler, which held the magical mirror and requested that he keep it safely until they were ready to leave Queen Sarah's palace.

The butler turned around and left, while Cynthia jiggled the door lock with the room keys.

As soon as she opened the door, everyone gasped in awe at the contemporary architecture of the guest house.

"This is so beautiful, I might faint!" Violet said.

"Wow! The guest house has a swimming pool!" Primrose squealed, jumping up and down.

"Cannonball!" Pepper yelled, jumping quickly onto the big fluffy white pillow on the ground.

"Oooooooh! This type of lavish kitchen has always been my dream kitchen, along with that pantry!" Pepper cried, racing to the pantry.

It was almost dusk, and the sun was setting in.

"Everyone, it is time to get ready and head out to the royal palace to attend Queen Sarah's marriage reception dinner, so please freshen up and get dressed, we'll leave for dinner soon," Hedwig announced.

After some time, everyone was decked out the stunning outfits that Queen Sarah's maids had arranged for them. When they were ready and assembled in the living room, everyone complimented each other on their fabulous dresses and looks.

Primrose was wearing a blue velvet gown, Violet was wearing a purple satin gown, Acorn was wearing a green-and-white polka-dot dress, Hedwig was wearing a crisp white shirt and black pants with brown suspenders, Pepper was wearing a floral dress with a white denim jacket, Jax was wearing a woolen black suit, Mrs. Walters was wearing a pink cotton gown decorated with snowy lace, and the triplet deer were wearing beautiful matching glittery golden gowns. The outfits were the perfect size and fit everyone just right.

Soon after they assembled in the living room, they went to the royal Sweet Palace ceremony hall that was right beside the garden.

The bride, Queen Sarah, was wearing a long, silky, flowy, white gown with a matching sheer veil.

She looked absolutely dazzling, standing next to the bridegroom who was dressed in a gray tuxedo.

The bridegroom was the prince of a neighboring kingdom.

Both the bride and groom looked gorgeous, posing on the dais for the photographers.

Everyone climbed the grand staircase leading to the dais to wish the newlyweds a happy marriage.

"Your highness, you both are looking fabulous and make such a great pair. On behalf of all the munchkins and woodland animals, I would like to congratulate you both, please have a happy married life," Mrs. Walters said, cheerfully.

"Thank you, Mrs. Walters!" Queen Sarah replied, giving her a hug.

The groom also thanked the group with a smile.

"You look gorgeous in this wedding gown, Queen Sarah!" Primrose congratulated, smiling.

"Thank you, sweetheart, you look pretty as well in this blue velvet gown!" Queen Sarah responded, back to Primrose's compliment.

After spending a few moments in the reception hall to get a glimpse of all the nicely dressed wedding guests, everyone headed towards the dining hall to enjoy the feast.

As soon as they were seated at the table, the servants came and started to serve mouthwatering various dishes such as broccoli cheddar soup, apple strudel, barbecue chips, crispy French fries, ricotta ravioli, garlic bread with hummus spread, spicy enchiladas, cheese pizza, cucumber sandwiches, steamed rice with boiled vegetables, and macaroni and cheese. For dessert, they served chocolate fondue, frosted sugar cookies, lemon meringue cheesecake, and cherry tarts.

Everyone had devoured the gigantic full-course dinner and it was already late night.

"Fellas, we need to go back to our room and catch some sleep, then we have to vacate the royal guest house early morning tomorrow and meet with Major Frederick, to plan our journey to Hellevue Island," Hedwig warned, seriously.

"Awwwww, but Hedwig…, I wanted to see the ballroom dancing happening soon! It's just not fair!" Susan whined, crossing her legs.

"Yeah, can't we stay a bit longer, Hedwig?" Acorn complained, agreeing with Susan's whining.

"Me too! I wanted to attend the midnight karaoke happening in half an hour," Violet cried, stomping up and down on her paws.

"I really wanted to check out the perfume samples they were giving at the courtyard. I love wearing strong scented perfumes," Pepper said, pouting and digging her paw into the red fluffy carpet.

"Enough whining and complaining, you guys! We're not here to entertain ourselves! We're supposed to be working on our mission! The more time we waste here, the more delayed our expedition is going to be. I wish we could stay a bit longer but I'm afraid we can't attend the ballroom dancing or the midnight karaoke event as it is already late and we have a big day tomorrow. I'm sorry, Susan, Pepper, Violet, and Acorn," Hedwig said, shaking his head with disapproval.

Everyone walked back to the royal guest house and changed into their warm fleece pajamas.

Primrose quickly changed into a sparkling rainbow nightgown and brushed her teeth with strawberry toothpaste.

As soon as they changed into their pajamas, everyone crashed into the canopy bed and fell asleep after a quick pillow fight, but the triplet deer found themselves drawn by the shiny moonlight, so they decided to sleep outside in the beautiful garden right next to the guest house, gazing at the starry night.

After a good sleep, they all woke up early in the morning and got ready to meet with Major Frederick before dawn.

Major Frederick arranged a big warship along with a few soldiers for the woodland animals to continue their journey to Hellevue Island. Since Major Frederick felt that combating Evelyn's eccentric army was too tough, he decided to volunteer himself for the journey along with a few of his most loyal soldiers.

"My dear friends, it was nice meeting you all. Have a safe and successful journey, and I wish the best of luck to you all in your efforts to conquer Evelyn and break the spell that she has cast upon humanity. I'm looking forward to meeting you all again on your successful return from Hellevue," Mrs. Walters said, while seeing off everyone.

"I'm going to miss you guys a lot. Have a safe journey, and goodbye for now," Jax added, giving Violet and everyone else a tight hug.

Epic Voyage to Murky Hellevue

The woodland animals and Primrose boarded the warship. Once everyone was aboard, the soldiers undocked the warship from its anchor and set sail across the ocean to Hellevue.

The warship was equipped with weapons to protect Primrose and the woodland animals from Evelyn's dangerous entourage.

After a few days of sailing, while the ship was in the middle of the ocean, a heavy wind from terrible stormy weather made the ship drift off course. Primrose and all the other woodland animals grew frightened a bit looking at the bad stormy weather.

"Sit tight and put on your life jackets everyone. It's possible the ship may drift into the whirlpool due to these strong tidal waves. We may need to jump ship to save ourselves in the event the ship sinks," Captain Leonard announced, handing out the life jackets to everyone onboard the ship.

Primrose got even more nervous and started praying.

"Merciful God! You must help us! Amen!" Primrose whispered to herself, quietly.

Captain Leonard with the help of a few of his crew members had managed to sail across the whirlpool and avoided the probable shipwreck that was about to occur.

"Oh, my goodness! Thankfully, nothing happened to the ship. Thank you, dear Captain Leonard," Violet yelled, clasping her paws together tightly.

As the weather conditions grew better,

the team continued the journey filled with happy chatter about sharing their experiences at Queen Sarah's marriage, making everyone feel slightly calmer.

Suddenly, a big rogue wave started to appear on the horizon. Captain Leonard started to lose control of the helm since the titanic tidal waves pushed more ocean water onto the ship, causing the ship to veer off course.

Captain Leonard struggled to grapple the helm and ship started to sink into ocean.

Everyone onboard the ship started to panic and worried that they may not make it alive.

"Mayday! Mayday! Brace yourself! The ship is about to sink, please wear life jackets and jump off the ship as the rogue wave will make the ship sink," Captain Leonard alerted, making a distress announcement.

"Sink or swim! Sink or swim!" Pepper screamed, freaking out.

"Cynthia and Ashlynn, you were both great sisters but it's time to say goodbye, I guess!" Susan shrieked, clutching her hooves together.

"Noooooooooooooooo! Are we going to die? I want to go back to Heavenvue!" Violet wailed, waving her paws in the air wildly.

"God, please help us! I want to go back home and see my family, before I die!" Primrose cried, sobbing into her hands.

Fortunately, Hedwig was the only one who was maintaining his cool.

"Calm down, everyone. Nobody is going to die and we're going to make it out of this difficult situation. Be resilient, our divine mystical power is bound to protect us all," Hedwig said, making everyone stress a bit less.

The soldiers helped Primrose and the woodland animals out on their life jackets and made them jump out of the ship via the emergency exit. Captain Leonard and the soldiers quickly gathered as many weapons as possible and loaded them onto the lifeboats and they too jumped off the ship to save their lives.

As soon as everyone jumped off the ship, the warship sank into the ocean.

Primrose and woodland animals were floating out in the open water with their life jackets on. Immediately, the soldiers began helping them climb onto the lifeboats.

Once everyone had been pulled into the lifeboats, Captain Leonard said:

"Alright everyone, by God's grace, we all survived this terrific storm. Our soldiers have managed to save some food supplies for the rest of our journey; they also managed to safeguard weapons to combat Evelyn's army. However, we lost our warship, so let's hope we don't hit with any more ocean storms until we make it to Hellevue Island.

We need to raft on these small boats for the next two to three days to reach Hellevue."

"Thank you, Captain Leonard, for saving our lives.

"We all truly appreciate your and the army soldiers' dedicated efforts to make it through this terrible situation and save all of us.

"In fact, our magical mirror is also safely rescued. Without it, we wouldn't be able to conquer the evil sorceress. We owe you one, big time!" Hedwig said, gratefully.

The boat journey continued for the next three sunsets without any hindrance from the weather.

"Hey, look over the horizon! I see an island! I believe it is Hellevue! Come on, let's see if it is, you guys!" Hedwig hollered, pointing his wing at the horizon, squinting his eyes.

Captain Leonard looked through his binoculars and gasped, his heart filling with awe.

"Right on! You are absolutely right, Hedwig! You really have some good eyesight. While we have almost made it to Hellevue, I have some bad news for you all. Looks like the island is heavily guarded by Evelyn's army. I can see many soldiers guarding the shore. We must come up with some a plan to attack and conquer Evelyn's army," Captain Leonard said, his heart suddenly filling with mixed feelings.

"Thank you, Captain Leonard, let me take the lead from here, we must prepare to carefully attack Evelyn's army and conquer them," Major Frederick, the head of the military, interjected.

Major Frederick and few other soldiers who accompanied the team on the orders of Queen Sarah to defeat Evelyn's army had a few active discussions onboard the boat, then came up with a perfect plan of attack.

"Listen up, folks, here's the plan. We'll try to invade Evelyn's kingdom tomorrow after the twilight since it will be easy to attack the enemy's army in the dark. Using the limited weapons that we rescued from the sunken ship, our soldiers will carefully attack those of Evelyn's soldiers who are guarding the sea shore. While our soldiers try to distract the enemy soldiers, Hedwig, Primrose, and the rest of the woodland animals team must somehow try to sneak into Evelyn's haunted castle without getting caught and try to remove Evelyn's evil casting powers using their mystical abilities and the magical mirror.

"Meanwhile, Captain Leonard will guard our boats and supplies," Major Frederick ordered, looking at everyone.

"That sounds like a great plan to me, don't you think?" Hedwig said, glancing around at everybody.

As soon as they reached the sea shore the next evening, they noticed a glimpse of dark, inky, sea shore that was heavily guarded by Evelyn's army soldiers. The island was shrouded by the murky atmosphere and its haze of gloomy clouds. Swarming all around the sea shore, a colony of bats was making scary shoal sounds.

Everyone on the boat quickly got into position for the plan.

They had their teeth clenched nervously and fidgeted impatiently.

"This place looks so scary and frightening, I just want to curl underneath my bed covers!" Primrose murmured to herself, nervously.

The Hellevue Annihilation and a Secret Passage

Moments later, the soldiers jumped off the lifeboats and started attacking the dangerous foe's army.

While the soldiers continued the battle, Primrose and all the woodland animals slowly got off the boats and sneaked up slyly towards the shore.

As the enemy army was completely engaged in fighting with Major Frederick and his army, a few soldiers of Major Frederick's army were able to help the woodland animals and Primrose get past the enemy army's visual line of sight and make their way to Evelyn's haunted castle through a secret passage.

Hedwig led the team in crawling through the secret passage.

The passage was damp and filled with silky white cobwebs. As they began to crawl, everyone started to create loud chaos.

"Owie!" Primrose yowled, sucking on her right thumb.

"Shhhhhh, Primrose! Quiet! Quiet! The enemies might hear us! What happened to your thumb?" Hedwig whisper-yelled, putting his wing over his firm beak.

"I think I got bitten by a spider. I feel some burning sensation on my right thumb," Primrose whimpered, sadly.

"You're going to be okay, Primrose. Just keep sucking your thumb for a bit, then you'll be fine," Violet advised, nodding in agreement.

By the time they reached the end of the tunnel, everyone heard a raspy voice coming from above:

"Miss Evelyn Velecrona, I'm afraid I have some bad news for you that we're being attacked by Heavenvue's military. Some of the lads of Heavenvue appear to have managed to enter our kingdom through some of our secret castle passages!"

"Guys, let's be quiet! I think this is the voice of Baxter, the personal assistant of Evelyn!" Hedwig whisper-announced, requesting everyone to remain silent.

"What?! This can't be happening in my kingdom! No one would dare attack Hellevue! Baxter, make an emergency announcement to our soldiers to kill any Heavenvue residents seen!" Evelyn screeched, her heart filling with rage.

"Yes, your honor! I will pass on your orders to all our soldiers!" Baxter replied, writing an emergency scroll.

Primrose and woodland animals quietly eavesdropped on the conversation between Evelyn and Baxter.

As they crawled even further in the secret passage, Cynthia discovered a large opening flap, which was covered with a sheer cloth.

"Um, I think I found an exit to get out of this secret passage! It looks like it's covered!" Cynthia said, tapping on the wall with her cloven hoof.

"Yes! Good work, Cynthia! But we have to figure out what's on the other side of the flap! If we get caught, Evelyn's soldiers might kill us!" Acorn exclaimed, munching on her paws nervously.

"I can go sneak into the exit and find out what's on the other side of the secret passage. I'm really good at spying!" Pepper volunteered, raising her paw.

"Good idea, Pepper! Please go ahead and do this for us! Let me give you my seashell whistle. If you are in any trouble, just blow on this seashell whistle and we'll come to rescue you. Also, we will wait right here until you return," Ashlynn said, handing her seashell whistle to Pepper.

Pepper grabbed the seashell whistle and quickly climbed through the large flap.

As Pepper slowly made her way out of the secret passage, she found that the passage exit actually opened up to Evelyn's bedroom. Inside the dark bedroom there was a big black canopy bed decorated with musty skulls. The room was lit by black candles hung in the chandelier. The walls of the bedroom were decorated with old creepy portraits of Evelyn's ancestors.

Pepper slowly scurried deeper into the dark bedroom and noticed that both Evelyn and Baxter were walking out of the bedroom.

Realizing the fact that nobody was there in Evelyn's bedroom at that moment, Pepper decided to dig up a big hole to make the passage exit larger for Primrose and others to quickly get into the bedroom through the opening flap.

"Listen up, everyone! Slowly come out of the passage exit, this passage actually opens up directly into Evelyn's bedroom. I don't see anyone in this bedroom at the moment, so let's jump right in and hide under the curtains," Pepper announced, quietly by lifting the opening flap of the passage.

Primrose and all other woodland animals crawled up into Evelyn's bedroom, then suddenly they all heard loud thumping of footsteps near the bedroom corridor.

"Shhh, looks like Evelyn's is coming back to her bedroom, everybody please hide out quickly wherever possible!" Primrose requested, to everyone.

Hedwig hid under the chandelier hanging near the dresser. Pepper and Acorn hid underneath the bed. The triplet deer hid behind the long black velvet drapes. Violet and Primrose hid inside Evelyn's closet.

Back at the shore, Major Frederick and his army continued battling against Evelyn's army and had managed to gain some level of control over the enemy's army.

A Blessing in Disguise

After Primrose and the team managed to conceal themselves in their hiding spots, Evelyn rushed back into her bedroom with Baxter sitting on her wrist. She stomped on the floor furiously, with her arms crossed tightly.

"I will not spare anyone from Heavenvue who dare to enter my territory. Baxter, let's go meet with our army commander to create an attack plan!" Evelyn snarled, pounding the dresser table with her magical wand and spellbook.

"You got it, Evelyn! Let's go kill'em!" Baxter replied, fanning her flames of fury.

Evelyn angrily hurried out of her bedroom to meet with her army commander, but she had mistakenly forgotten to take her magical wand and spellbook with her.

Once Evelyn and Baxter could no longer be heard down the hallway, everyone quickly jumped out of their hiding spots and whisper-squealed happily, like a pack of cheerful mice.

"Wow, Evelyn actually left her wand and spellbook! What if we use them to learn and cast spells?" Primrose said, giddily.

"Absolutely, it's actually a blessing in disguise! It makes our job of breaking your curse, I mean the curse on humanity cast by Evelyn even easier, Primrose," Hedwig replied, clapping with his wings, joyfully.

Hedwig continued saying, "I want you to quickly read through her spellbook, find the right spell, and look for details on how to apply it on her, so that we can put an end to Evelyn's wicked casting powers and break the curse. There should definitely be some spell that will enable us to achieve our goal."

Primrose grabbed the muddy-splotched spellbook, flipped through all the pages, glanced through the entire spellbook and quickly figured out how she could take over Evelyn's power.

There were many good and bad magical spells described in the spellbook. Some of the good spells that Primrose found in the book included turning villages into paradises, making old people young, making sages immortal, resurrecting people from the dead who did great deeds when they were alive and many more such good spells. The spellbook also had some funny spell powers like turning naughty mice into cheese and turning convicted prisoners into rotten eggs.

"I think I found the perfect spell for our plan!" Primrose said, looking at everyone.

"Wow! That's amazing quick reading skills you've got there!" Susan exclaimed in awe.

"Thank you, Susan! Here is the spell I found that we should use on Evelyn.

"If I hold Evelyn's wand in one hand and also hold Hedwig's magical mirror in the other hand at the same time, the moment Evelyn sees her face reflecting in the mirror, immediately her physical body will start to dissipate and her evil casting powers will also get relinquished—but there is a catch," Primrose said, thoughtfully.

"What is the catch? Could you help us understand?" Violet asked, nervously.

"Yeah, Primrose! What's the catch?" Pepper voiced, nodding in agreement with Violet.

"Well, as soon as Evelyn's face starts disappearing on the magical mirror, all her evil powers will be vanished into thin air, but at the same time I may gain colossal superhuman powers that must be blocked from being exploited for my own selfish desires. My superhuman powers must be carefully watched to make sure I avoid any human mistakes that I may be prone to make. The good news is that Hedwig has the ability to block my mystical powers, but he can only do it once we get back to Heavenvue. So, please keep in mind that

Hedwig can't use his magical powers while we are on Hellevue.

"I must be careful with my supposedly acquired supernatural human powers until we head back to the good island side of Mystopical. This is the catch, pals!" Primrose claimed, pointing at the spell in Evelyn's spellbook.

"This is amazing! Thank you, Primrose, for all the information! We, all the woodland animals place our trust in you, and we're sure that you won't misuse your prospective magical human powers for any such unconscionable reasons. However, we'll likely let you use your potential mystical abilities to protect the welfare of Mystopical population, heal the cursed people and animals, cure your father's health, and more importantly resurrect your dead mother's life," Hedwig said, happily.

"Thank you, Hedwig! It means a lot to me, especially what you just said right now," Primrose said, her heart filling with ecstasy and contentment.

"You are most welcome, Primrose," Hedwig said, nodding his head.

While Primrose and woodland animals continued the conversation, suddenly they all heard a loud thumping of footsteps of Evelyn again.

"Everybody, go back to your hiding spots immediately and camouflage yourself like a chameleon as best as you can! Looks like Evelyn is coming back to her bedroom. I will hold her wand and our magical mirror and stand right behind the door and show the mirror right to her face as soon as she opens the door," Primrose urged, panicky.

"Remember, Primrose you must be audacious and be vigilant! Any small mistake you make in front of Evelyn may jeopardize our plan and put us all at risk," Hedwig cautioned.

"Certainly Hedwig, you can trust me. I won't let you down," Primrose responded to Hedwig, strongly expressing her confidence and bravery.

Demise of Evelyn Velecrona

Evelyn and Baxter (sitting on Evelyn's arm) walked up to the bedroom, kick-opening the door, and saw Primrose standing right in front of her.

"Who are you, miserable human, and how dare you enter my bedroom?" Evelyn shouted, her hands balled into fierce fists.

"I'm Primrose Fernetise, me and my friends, the woodland animals, are here to save the world from you and your evil curse, Evelyn Velecrona!" Primrose yelled, glaring into her terrifying eyes.

As Primrose responded to Evelyn, Hedwig and all the other woodland animals quickly came out of their hiding spots and stood behind Primrose.

"Your evil powers will cease to exist, you better surrender yourself and save your life or else you will pay the price, Evelyn!" Pepper proclaimed, moving to stand next to Primrose.

"How dare you ask me to surrender, you stupid stinky skunk! Give me back my wand right now or I will kill all of you!" Evelyn screamed, quickly trying to snatch her wand from Primrose's hand.

The woodland animals were standing behind and backing her up at that critical moment, which had boosted up Primrose's audacity.

"Never, that's not going to happen with us, dear sorceress!" Primrose yelled sarcastically, jerking her hand away from Evelyn.

As Evelyn harshly attempted to yank her wand from Primrose's hand, she immediately lifted the magical mirror and pointed towards Evelyn's face.

"I dare you to take a closer look in the mirror and realize how wicked and sinful you look!" Primrose screamed, staring at Evelyn right in her face.

Evelyn shrieked loudly and tried to look away from the magical mirror, but Primrose had managed to force Evelyn to see her horrified look in the mirror and kept the wand away from Evelyn's reach.

Within a few minutes, little beads of sweat and tears dripped down Evelyn's face, turning pale and she started shivering.

"No, you can't do this to me!" Evelyn cried, with a trembling voice as she collapsed onto the floor.

"Please stop it, you dumb crazy creatures! You can't steal my queen's casting powers!" Baxter screeched, flitting in panic all around Evelyn's bedroom.

As Evelyn collapsed, her body slowly began to crumble and vanish into thin air. At the same time, Baxter also started to fade away.

Suddenly, a sparkling flash of lightning appeared in the sky followed by a loud rumbling thunder. Primrose looked at it and turned into an angel with a glittery silk white gown and matching wings, along with a shiny golden halo, singing joyfully.

"Wow! What an exuberant moment! I can feel positive energy everywhere!" Violet cheered, filled with awe and wonder.

"Yup! We nailed it!" Pepper hollered, squinting her eyes.

Primrose flushed with pride as her friends congratulated her on her victory over the evil spirits.

Everyone hugged each other joyfully and celebrated the special moment.

"Great victory, everyone! Congratulations, Primrose, on your newly acquired mystical powers. The curse on humanity that was cast by Evelyn has formally been lifted.

"Okay, you guys. Coming back to the important point, Primrose, let me emphasize that you must remember to use your mystical abilities wisely only upon approval from us, the divine powered woodland animals!" Hedwig exclaimed, wagging his wing back and forth in Primrose's face.

"Thank you, Hedwig! Of course, I won't let you down by misusing my mystical powers!" Primrose replied, expressing complete agreement.

"Since our epic expedition to Hellevue and the task of defeating Evelyn is over, we should plan our return journey to the other part of Mystopical, Heavenvue. Let's all head back to the shore to meet with Captain Leonard and Major Frederick to start our voyage back home," Pepper said, pointing at the ocean view across Evelyn's bedroom window.

Everyone agreed with what Pepper had said and started towards the sea shore.

"Welcome back, fellas! Congratulations on your accomplishment, our soldiers have successfully wiped out Evelyn's entire army as well. Great victory to all of us!" Major

Frederick cheered, wiping his sweaty forehead.

"Yes, I second the victory, congratulations everyone! Now let's figure out a way to get back to Munchville," Captain Leonard added, clapping joyfully.

"Thank you, Captain Leonard and Major Frederick, and to all of you Munchville soldiers for your support!" Primrose cheered, pumping her fists into the air.

Hedwig and all the woodland animals also thanked them, giving them tight hugs.

"But how are we going to get back home since we lost our ship?" Acorn asked, anxiously.

"Good question, Acorn, I have already made a plan for this. Since the Munchville soldiers conquered Hellevue, all warships of this island now belong to Munchville, specifically to Majesty Queen Sarah. So, we'll be using one of the ships of Hellevue for our voyage back to Munchville," Captain Leonard responded, firmly.

"Sounds like a great plan to me, Captain Leonard!" Acorn replied, smiling.

The Journey Back Home

Everyone boarded the ship and started their voyage back to Munchville.

"Hey, um what about food for the journey? I'm starving!" Violet asked, rubbing her grumbling stomach.

"I've got you covered with just one tiny carrot, my little muncher! I hope that takes care of your volcano for the rest of your journey," Captain Leonard answered, sarcastically in a jovial manner.

"What? Just one measly carrot? That's how much a baby rabbit eats in one meal!" Violet exclaimed, gasping in shock.

"Just kidding! Violet, me, Major Frederick and the army actually collected some food from Evelyn's castle pantry that should be enough for all of us to make the journey back home. I hope we don't run into any bad weather again on the way home and get stalled in the middle of the ocean without food supplies," Captain Leonard replied, chuckling to himself.

The others thanked Captain Leonard for assuring them with food and were having a hoot of laughter about Violet's anxious craving behavior.

Due to Primrose's newly acquired mystical powers, the woodland animals, Munchville army, Major Frederick and Captain Leonard managed to sail safely through the harsh ocean weather conditions.

After a few days of sailing, they finally made it to the eastern shore of Heavenvue.

Captain Leonard docked the ship on the Sweet Palace harbor and ordered everyone to disembark from the ship.

Queen Sarah arranged a grand welcome party in honor of Primrose and the team's great triumph over Evelyn and breaking the evil curse cast by her.

Primrose and the woodland animals had a great time celebrating their success with Queen Sarah, Major Frederick, Captain Leonard and all the other munchkins who attended the party, along with Mrs. Walters and Jax who were also invited by Queen Sarah.

Everyone enjoyed the teriyaki tofu, grilled marshmallows, corn on the cob, boiled broccoli, veggie tamales, zucchini casseroles, and peach gelato as a dessert, which was perfect for the moonlight dinner party. Violet almost had a stomach ache since she munched all the carrots kept on the platter.

Primrose and the woodland animals stayed overnight at the same royal guest house where they stayed earlier when they first visited Munchville.

This time around, the triplet deer, Ashlynn, Susan, and Cynthia, who slept previously in the beautiful palace garden grounds, decided they would sleep inside the guest house, since it was freezing cold outside.

The next morning, after saying goodbye to Mrs. Walters, Jax, and all the other munchkins, Primrose and the woodland animals continued their journey back to Amiablevue in their wooden boat, sailing down the blue river.

"Listen up, everybody! I have a quick announcement to make," Hedwig proclaimed, clearing his throat.

Everyone quickly spun around, giving Hedwig their full attention.

"We'll sail back to the shore near the dense forest on the outskirts of Amiablevue, where we met Primrose for the first time. Then, we'll see Primrose off and let her walk back home to reunite with her family. Afterwards, we have some assignments to do in the dense forest of Amiablevue for a few days before we voyage back to Heavenvue Island."

"Sounds like a good plan, but what kind of assignments do we have in the forest, Hedwig?" Violet asked, giving him a curious look.

"Well, it's about planning our next expedition with Primrose, Violet," Hedwig replied, stretching his wings.

"I see, but what about Primrose?" Violet asked, curiously.

"I'm afraid Primrose can't attend our meeting because she must go back home and reunite with her family as she was away from them for a while. Her family misses her badly.

"We will meet you sometime soon and discuss our next expedition, Primrose," Hedwig said, rubbing his beak with his wing.

"I'm totally fine with your plan, Hedwig. In fact, I'm eagerly waiting to see my mother!" Primrose said, jumping up and down at the thought of her beloved mother.

Her emotions and feelings were filled with joy.

Farewell for Now

$\mathbf{A}$s everyone continued their chatty conversions, their boat finally arrived at the Amiablevue outskirts. Everyone jumped off the boat and hugged Primrose with hearts filled with overwhelmed joy and happiness.

"Thank you all for everything you have done. I'm so proud to have you all as my new best friends. I can't express enough in words how grateful I am for your help. I going to miss you guys a lot, and I'm sorry I didn't believe your story when we met! Please forgive me for my ignorance!" Primrose said, crying joyfully.

"Awwwwwwww! Not at all, my new bestie! Any human kiddo who would have encountered such a situation like this with unusual talking animals would have done the same.

"In fact, you were brave and kind enough to come to a point of realization quickly and build trust in us. We are going to miss you too, Primrose!" Susan said, touched by Primrose's kind words.

Soon enough, everyone seconded Susan's words and started to shed tears filled with an overwhelming friendship.

"All right, everybody! Listen up! Here is the moment of truth, Primrose. With the combination of your mystical powers and our blessings, your dead mother has been brought back to life and your father's sickness has been healed.

"Also, the wellness of nations will thrive going forward and more importantly, the curse on humanity has been broken. The humans, animals, and plants will flourish in the entire Mystopical even in your beloved Amiablevue land as well. I'm glad we could bring back joy, peace, and happiness to the world.

"I really appreciate our achievement so far!

"I'm going to restrain your mystical powers for now. However, we will be able to reinstate your mystical powers in the future, if necessary to save the world from evil spirits once again.

"But I need one promise from you, Primrose," Hedwig said, cautiously.

"Sure, certainly Hedwig, tell me what promise you need from me," Primrose responded, quickly looking at Hedwig seriously.

"You should never disclose your mystical powers or about our expedition to defeat Evelyn in Hellevue to anyone in your family and friends, especially the general population of Amiablevue," Hedwig said, crossing his wings tightly.

"Of course, Hedwig, you can trust me! Your faith in me means everything and it's an honor to me! I will never disclose this highly confidential information to anyone, including my family!" Primrose said, showing optimism and confidence.

Primrose hugged each and every woodland animal, then she instantaneously had her heavy heart filled with more mixed feelings about missing her best friends and at the same time, the joy of reuniting with her beloved family.

Primrose continued her lonely journey back home through the dense forest.

Primrose's Reunion with her Family

As Primrose walked through the forest, everything on her path looked so wondrous, the forest birds' chirps were soothing to her ears, the flowers all around the thick grassy pathway were filled with colors and pleasant sweet aromas making her feel exuberant.

After walking through the forest for a while full of excitement and a bit of nervousness, Primrose saw an exquisitely beautiful mansion at some distance away from her.

She walked further and noticed her brother, Stanley, standing next to Ginger.

"Wait a minute. Is this my house? This can't be, or is it?" Primrose thought, softly tapping her chin.

She started to walk briskly and as she went closer, Primrose noticed her father and mother also standing beside the dark brown wagon parked near the wooden front porch.

Primrose's emotions burst into tears and ran into her parents' arms.

"Mother! Father! Stanley! Ginger! I missed you all so much!" Primrose yelled, hugging her mother tightly and shedding tears, her heavy heart felt lighter with joy and happiness.

"Primrose! I'm so happy to see you, my sweetheart! We searched everywhere for you for many days! Where were you? We all missed you so much, honey," Primrose's mother cried with her heart filled with overjoy, wrapping her arms tightly around Primrose.

"Yeah, where were you, Primrose? We were out looking for you for days!" Stanley asked, anxiously.

"Well, I went to the other side of the dense forest to find nectar from the divine flower in the deep forest. Then, somehow I got lost on the way back due to heavy rain in the forest. Anyway, it's so good that I'm back, and I'm happy to see you all again!" Primrose answered, lying a bit to conceal the truth about her expedition with the woodland animals to save humanity.

While Primrose was making her way back to her home to reunite with her family, to avoid any confusion for Stanley and Primrose's father about the uncommon revival of her dead mother's existence, the woodland animals had actually erased some of their past memories to make both of them believe that Primrose's mother had never died before.

The same thing for Primrose's mother, her memory was also made completely unaware about her death and she didn't remember anything about what had happened before.

"Primrose, my child, we all missed you so much, I worried a lot about you. Every night, I had nightmare about what would happen to you being alone in the wild forest. By God's grace, we are so happy to see you back home safely!

"Please promise me you will never go alone to the deep forest anymore!" Primrose's father said, his voice filled with concern.

"Sure, Father. I promise not to go alone into the forest, anymore! By the way, I'm afraid I couldn't find the nectar for you, but I see that your legs seem recovered, am I right? Also, what happened to our old wooden cottage, how did you guys manage to build this gigantic mansion?!" Primrose said surprised, hugging him tightly.

Primrose's father nodded and hugged Primrose back.

"Yes honey, by God's grace both my paralyzed legs were healed and about your question about the mansion, a few more miraculous things have actually happened indeed, while you were away from all of us.

"I will tell you everything in detail, but you must be tired and starving without home cooked food for many days!

"Please freshen up, let's discuss everything over lunch," Primrose's father said, happily.

"Primrose, I'll make your favorite foods, beans and franks along with my specialty chocolate tiramisu for a dessert, would that be okay with you?" Primrose's mother asked, smiling.

"Sure, Mother. I'd love to eat that for lunch," Primrose replied, excitedly.

"All right, it's settled then! Let me start cooking and you go get ready for lunch," Primrose's mother said, gleefully.

Primrose took out a set of new clothes from her bedroom closet and started to walk towards the fresh water pond next to her house.

"Where are you going, Primrose?" Primrose's father asked, scratching his head.

"I'm going to the pond nearby to take a bath, Father," Primrose replied, clutching her dress tightly.

"As I have mentioned earlier, a few incredible changes have happened to us in our family lifestyle also, I will explain to you later about everything.

"But for now, you no longer need to go to nearby pond to bathe.

"We have built a new bathroom in this new mansion with a beautiful bathtub as well for you to bathe and play in the water," Primrose's father said, pointing out the bathroom to her.

"Wow, that is awesome! I'm so excited to bathe and play in this bathtub!" Primrose responded, enthusiastically.

"I know sweetheart, I have already filled the tub with hot water and lavender bath bombs for you to use. I will let you have fun with your bathtub.

"While you get ready, I will go feed some carrots and hay to Ginger in her stable stall."

Primrose went to bathroom and played in the hot water bathtub for a while. After finishing a relaxing and refreshing bath, she dressed up and got ready for lunch.

As soon as Primrose had gotten ready for lunch, it was already freshly plated on the table.

"Lunch is almost ready, honey. I'm not sure where Father and Stanley are. By the way, you are looking pretty in that blue dress, Primrose!" Primrose's mother complimented, arranging the crockery and water glasses on the dining table.

"Thank you, Mother. Let me go find Father and Stanley. I think they are in the barn feeding Ginger because that's what Father said to me earlier when I was going to take a bath," Primrose said, looking out the window.

Primrose walked out to the horse stable stall behind the mansion, in the corner of the backyard.

Primrose saw Stanley and her father ripping hay with their hands and feeding it to Ginger.

"Ginger! I missed you so much! How are you, my cutie pie?" Primrose yelled, running towards Ginger and wrapping her arms around her neck.

Ginger neighed to express her contentment to Primrose and rubbed herself against Primrose's soft cheeks.

"Hey, Primrose! Would you like to feed some carrots to Ginger?" Stanley asked, handing Primrose a handful of carrots.

"I'd love to, Stanley," Primrose replied, taking the carrots out of Stanley's hands.

Primrose fed Ginger all the carrots she was holding in her hands.

"Father! Stanley! Come on, let's go eat lunch. Mother is calling us for lunch," Primrose said, cupping her hands together around her mouth.

"Of course, sweetie. I'm starving! Let's go eat lunch," Primrose's father said, carrying a bucket filled with carrots back to the mansion.

Everyone sat around the dining table and began to devour their beans and franks dish.

By the time they had finished their scrumptious main course meal, Primrose's mother came running from the kitchen with the chocolate tiramisu for dessert.

"Thank you, Mother, for preparing us this savory dish, it was really delicious! Please come join us also," Primrose said, licking her spoon.

"I will, dear," Primrose's mother replied, cutting the chocolate tiramisu dessert into small slices.

Everyone enjoyed their delicious lunch then Primrose suddenly remembered her father promising to share his story after lunch.

"Hey, Father! Can you please tell me now, what miraculous changes have happened to us in our family lifestyle while I was away? How did you all end up rebuilding a mansion out of our old small wooden cottage we had in such a short span of time?" Primrose asked, dabbing her mouth with a napkin.

"Sure, Primrose. Thanks for reminding me about that, I nearly forgot about that. I will tell you right now," Primrose's father replied, clearing his throat.

Then, he began to tell Primrose about what happened.

While Primrose was away on her undisclosed expedition with the woodland animals, Primrose's parents and Stanley found a treasure box buried in their rose garden, along with a corroded bronze key to unlock it.

The treasure box was full of gold and silver nuggets from an ancient civilization. The found treasure helped them come out of their poverty and renovate their small wooden cottage into a large beautiful mansion.

The wealth from the treasure they found had also helped Primrose's father start a lumberyard in Amiablevue. Timber trading from Primrose's father's lumberyard was good enough to take care of their family expenses.

As the Fernetise family finances prospered, Primrose and Stanley no longer had to do wood chopping and crocheting work to help take care of their family expenses.

Primrose and her family lived a joyful and blissful life happily ever after, forever.

To be continued…...

Can't wait to read what will happen next with Primrose and the woodland animals? Wondering what adventures they will go on next? Stay tuned and be on the lookout for our next book titled ***Primrose's Destiny!***

---- Kiara Shankar & Vinay Shankar ----

www.vikipublishing.com

Primrose's Destiny

An Audacious Girl Destined to Save Earth

KIARA SHANKAR
VINAY SHANKAR

KIARA SHANKAR

Primrose's Destiny

VINAY SHANKAR

All About the Author(s):

Kiara Shankar is a middle schooler from a small town in California, USA. Apart from writing books, she loves reading, artwork, writing poems, playing with her friends, and listening to her favorite Bollywood music. Kiara's poem "A Deadly Star" was published in the national level writing contest book "A Celebration of Poets" (Fall 2018 Edition - published by Creative Communication, Utah, USA).

Vinay Shankar is Kiara's dad, a software professional, who found himself inspired by his daughter's idea of writing fictional fairy tale books and decided to co-write books with her. This collaborative effort of the family is helping to bring great ideas to life!

A Deadly Star

I might be bright, with all my might, on this majestic starry night.

I bloom with gloom every night, granting wishes on dinner dishes of grilled fishes that come true from slimy dew into wonderful brew.

With my colorful colors and lovely lovers, my very own beautiful cast turns into a remarkable past and as I slowly fade away from my few million years in fusion, with my strong late faith, while churning and burning as hard as bold gold, but very old as it dies in honor mention, of my beloved worshiped master who soon became the milky white Moon.

Now, here my destiny in tiny Cordova, Alaska, will burst loudly like an exploding firecracker, with my big bright supernova, one fine night, when the whole daring human-being generation will be drinking Earth's fresh organic produced grapevine wine, right in front of their own small gifted eyes, to see how grateful I am for my very own supportive gigantic world.

— A poem by Kiara Shankar

CPSIA information can be obtained
at www.ICGtesting.com
Printed in the USA
LVHW051145250319
611720LV00012B/319/P

9 781950 263004